"What does it mean to hold power in this moment, a power that is born from old wealth, from capital, from corrupting influence? What does it mean for that power to seduce and entrance, to invite into the realm of the mystical and the ordinary? Naomi Telushkin explores these questions with prose that is as vital as her main character, Ayala. *Coats* as a novella is uniquely shaped and derives its own power from the mystery of Rabbi Nachman's verses and from the sure hand of a remarkably gifted writer."

—**Jai Chakrabarti**, author of *A Small Sacrifice for an Enormous Happiness* and *A Play for the End of the World*

"Naomi Telushkin's *Coats* reads like a geopolitical thriller in miniature, deftly weaving together threads of global politics, religious identity, erotic possibility, and more into a story of rich emotional ambiguity set amid seemingly immovable forces and perhaps impossible desires. A fantastic read that you won't soon forget."

—**Matt Bell**, author of *Appleseed*

"With the compression of poetry and the breathtaking pace of a political thriller, Naomi Telushkin tells parallel stories of violence: the violence of a passionate extramarital affair, over decades, as the narrator experiences this, and the political violence of an oppressive regime, as inflicted upon its journalists and intellectuals. There is violence, too, in the disintegration of childhood faith and decades-long love. I marveled at the richness of these pages and look forward to reading more from her soon. "

—**Chaya Bhuvaneswar**, author of *White Dancing Elephants: Stories*, a finalist for the PEN/Robert W. Bingham Prize for Debut Short Story Collection

COATS

Naomi Telushkin

Copyright © 2024 Naomi Telushkin. All rights reserved.

No part of this book may be reproduced in any form or by any electronic or mechanical means including information storage and retrieval systems, without permission in writing from the author. The only exception is by a reviewer, who may quote short excerpts in a review.

Published in the United States of America by *The Masters Review*
www.mastersreview.com

ISBN 979-8-9882557-7-2

Book interior by Julianne Johnson.
Cover by Emelie Mano.

For my mother and father,
who taught me everything about writing.

Editor's Note

For this year's Chapbook contest, we read through dozens of submissions, and because so many of them blew our socks off, it wasn't easy to choose the shortlist. But *Coats* stood out to all three of us from the very beginning and we came back to it over and over again.

The story is structured around a fable of the blessings of seven beggars given to a Jewish boy and girl who have fled Ukraine. With this, we have the weight of the past woven into the tension of the present, the sense that not everything is not as it seems, and the knowledge that most fables don't end well for someone.

And, oh, the story. A long-term affair nearing its painful end, the beautiful coats (so real I could feel them on my shoulders) used as leverage, a protagonist following her heart, even as it leads her into more and more unhappiness.

Naomi Telushkin's prose is confident throughout this piece. In every description, scene, and dialogue exchange, you'll feel you're in good hands.

—*Jen Dupree*
assistant editor

Introduction

While reading for this year's *Masters Review* chapbook contest, I was stunned by the quality of the shortlisted entries. Each manuscript was a pleasure to read, animated by an individual spark of brilliance that made it seem incomparable to every other. At first, choosing a winner felt impossible.

But then I remembered that I would be writing this introduction.

In my mind, the introduction to a book is written by a close friend, a biographer, or an academic scholar of the author, someone with a personal relationship to the text. Knowing nothing about these writers, I asked myself which manuscript I wanted to engage with that deeply, that could stand up to the scrutiny of study, that I could endorse with the passion of a friend. Which chapbook did I want to read over and over, certain I'd find new insights each time? Which text seemed that rich, that layered, that complex?

Coats by Naomi Telushkin was the undeniable answer. The novella opens almost essayistically, relating information about an actual historical figure, Rabbi Nachman of Breslov, and I was immediately struck by the wry, harshly irreverent voice: "[H]e wanted, *demanded*, that his followers be joyous… They were impoverished Jews in remote villages in early nineteenth century Ukraine. It wasn't a joyous time."

This is how we're introduced to Alexa, née Ayala, as she learns about Nachman on a Jewish Young Professionals trip to Kyiv. From the jump, she's disruptive and disdainful, obsessive and conflicted—a protagonist who challenged and intrigued me immediately. Within the first few pages, the text nests again, down another layer, transporting us into one of Nachman's tales, the Seven Beggars, reimagined as a terrifying haunting, a parable of trauma and refugee displacement:

> "[T]he bride and groom were forced to remember those days in the forest. Forced to remember what they'd shoved down and forgotten. How their breath turned to crystal, how screams wove around the trees, how his mother, nineteen, lay motionless in the snow, how her father said, 'leave her!' because they were still being hunted…
>
> The bride and groom clung to each other, awash in memories and blood, and they screamed at the beggars to stop it, but the beggars wouldn't go away. They never go away again."

The seven beggars' blessings—treated by the story as curses—structure the rest of the book, as it moves from Kyiv to Washington, DC, St. Petersburg, and New York City, following a decades-long affair between Alexa and a married man from her youth, dancing nonlinearly through time. The first scenes we see of this propulsive, toxic romance are written in appropriately short and brutal fragments, like scattered shards of glass. The setting of a Japanese restaurant is boiled down to a "a single orchid, a black vase. The sashimi bright, severe." I was blown away by the range and elegance of these varied constructions, how confidently the author moves between them.

The affair poisons how Alexa sees everything—how she interprets history, religion, art, other people's lives, her own life, her work, herself. But Coats has more expansive concerns, a sophisticated understanding of power at every level: between men and women, between classes, between nations, the money that runs the world. Alexa's story is firmly embedded in the now, the most urgent present, where the choices you make can get someone killed on the other side of the globe, where our most private and intimate desires can't be separated from the weight of the past and a world on fire. Reading it, I was thrilled, enlightened, discomfited, and devastated. I know you will be, too.

— *Kim Fu*
Author of *Lesser Known Monsters of the 21st Century*,
The Lost Girls of Camp Forevermore, and
For Today I Am a Boy

Coats

MODERN SCHOLARS ASSUME RABBI NACHMAN of Breslov was bipolar. He was moody, certainly, chaotic and turbulent, a man prone to violent and unhinged despair. And yet he wanted, *demanded*, that his followers be joyous.

It was hard for Nachman's followers to be joyous. They were impoverished Jews in remote villages in early nineteenth century Ukraine. It wasn't a joyous time. Jews spent their days getting stabbed by pitchforked Cossacks and their nights escaping under a full, frozen moon to America. They married in silence and in the dead of night, breaking glass under ice-laden chuppahs, so Cossack neighbors couldn't find them. They weren't happy but Rabbi Nachman insisted on it. And so they tried everything for his sake; they tried to be celebratory and light.

Rabbi Nachman's followers are particularly interesting because they refused to appoint a new leader after he died. Unlike other dynastic Chasidic communities, Breslov Chasids hold Nachman forever as their leader, and they speak and consult with him as though he is alive. Known colloquially as the Dead Chasidim, they'd invented an ecstatic, rapturous prayer, praying fervently, joyously for generations with Dead-but-Alive Nachman, wearing robes of all white.

We were told all this on a heritage trip to Kyiv, a trip I severely regretted applying for once I was on it. I'd been to Ukraine multiple times for work with the Aspen Institute. Why did I need to go again with "Jewish Young Professionals," a group as horrible, as sanitized as that sounds? It was run by a philanthropy organization that paid for our flights and accommodation. On the flight over, I tried to make small talk with the Jewish Young Professionals, tried to pretend like I wasn't above them, but my disdain inevitably crept in, and I drove them all away. They were eagerly, openly Jewish, their Judaism light and inoffensive, slipping in easily alongside their first law jobs and college sororities, while my Judaism was heavy, rule laden, tied to dark tradition. And so I smiled and failed to fit in, uncomfortably aware that this all-Jewish everything everywhere must be your—I mean *Isaac's*—whole life. (I was trying to stop narrating everything to you in my head, trying to accept we were finally finished, finite.)

The heritage excursion to Breslov and the details about Nachman intrigued me, however, much more than I expected. I too was in an obsessive, all-consuming relationship with a Dead Man. Isaac had a wife and three sons and a holiday house for their weekends in the Florida Keys, but was full of lifeless, comatose commitments for me—telling me over the phone, in a stolen moment at his son's birthday, that there would one day be a diamond on my hand, a child in my arms.

And so I thought, my interest piqued as we wandered through the abandoned, overrun Breslov village, the eerie, silent forests where the Dead Chasidim began, that maybe my instinct to go on this trip, an instinct which had failed to illuminate itself all week, would now finally make sense. I would learn new things about my heritage, my faith-driven past, that would inform my present. I would discover my ageless ancestors' wisdom and I would know what to do about Isaac next.

But there was nothing else. As the rest of the trip to Kyiv went on, listless, inconsequential, nothing grabbed me or opened up new connections like the Dead Chasidim. We were taken to the ballet, the opera, the synagogue. We ate borscht and pierogi. We met ancient Jews, Jews who'd spent a lifetime defined by their religion (barred entry to universities, barred exit visas to Israel) and yet barely understanding what exactly it all was. The Soviet Union had crushed the knowledge of religion out of them but they held onto artifacts (a tallis, a Torah, candlesticks) which they displayed in their bare homes. I had no idea why I was there. I'd told people I was taking this trip because of my Ukrainian parents, the Chasidic Jews on the perimeter of my family tree, that the language practice would enhance my position at the think tank in DC. What I didn't say was that it was Isaac's Russian parents, St. Petersburg-bred, glacial and imposing, that initially pushed me to learn the Cyrillic alphabet. What I didn't say was that I learned snatches of Russian secretly listening in on Isaac's calls with his oligarch father; desperate, teenaged calls where Isaac tried to impress him but his father refused to be impressed. I didn't say that Isaac had snuck me into his bedroom when we were fifteen and used me in silence so his housekeeper wouldn't hear. I didn't say that Isaac spoke to me in the hospital hallway after his first son was born, telling me in a shaky voice that it had to be over now, that he had just held his son's hand. We met in our hotel the week after Tali gave birth to his second; I'd bought us champagne after his third.

On Saturday afternoon, they split us up in two groups to have a "real Shabbat experience." The group leaders announced, cheerful, that we would have lunch in local Chasidic households, and the group participants clapped. My metaphoric teenage self recoiled, instantly wary of this imposed religious meal, and the Chasidic man they sent me to that afternoon summed me and my recoiling up in an instant. He invited us into his palatial four-story apartment, eight children running up and down the staircase, and his eyes lingered on me, the last to walk in, bristling with past injustices I couldn't convey.

There was something immediately between me and the Chasidic man, a shimmering hostility, and we both sensed it as the group made their pitchy, corporatized introductions. We sensed it as he instructed us to wash our hands before blessing the bread, sensed it as he led us in prayer over the wine. And we sensed it between us as the meal went on and on. While the other Jewish Young Professionals were deferential and small-talky and polite, I became drunk, hostile and aggressive, and as everyone spoke in bright, corporate tones about how *interesting* learning about the Dead Chasidim all was, I announced, abrupt, my absolute disdain for them. The table fell silent.

"You seemed really interested in them on the day," someone in the group finally offered, but I refused to give the Chasidic man his victory.

"No," I said. "I find it a ridiculous way to live."

The Chasidic man's wife looked down and then away. The Chasidic man however, said nothing but pointed to a portrait above my head. It was an oil painting of Rabbi Nachman of Breslov. The silence lingered on and on.

After the lunch, everyone mingled around the apartment with ginger tea and thick dessert wine and admired the city views. I decamped to the small, silent library on the third floor. I needed to hide, to be alone, and I distracted myself by practicing languages, scanning book titles in Hebrew, Russian, and Ukrainian. As I read the final one, the door creaked open. It was him.

The Chasidic man crept up to me and asked, the dull winter light dying in the windowpanes behind us, if I knew that the Dead Chasidim were famous for their stories. I said no, I didn't. And he told me that perhaps if I knew their stories, I wouldn't be so dismissive of them. I told him, perhaps. And then he clutched my arm (or did I imagine that? Chasidic men couldn't touch any woman but their wife) and he told me Nachman's stories were famous and complicated and almost indecipherable. They were like fairy tales but more beautiful and like myths but more symbolic, and as entertaining as any popular novel except they were transmitted to him through God. And the Chasidic man told me that he would tell me one, and we should see if even I, so arrogant, so university-educated, could possibly decipher it.

The sun set and the door swung firmly shut (and Chasidic men aren't allowed to shut doors in a room with a woman who isn't their wife), but he didn't leave, and he didn't move.

"Okay," I said finally. "Okay."

෴ ෴ ෴

ONE DAY AN ENTIRE JEWISH village had to flee Ukraine. They were discovered *yet again*, they were hated *yet again*, and so the village had to pack up and run. They fled into the icy forest, gleaming and lethal, and a boy child and a girl child wandered off from their families and disappeared into the blood-laced snow (because in this kind of fairy tale, not everyone makes it). Starving and lost, they encountered a blind beggar who gave them bread. They ate happily but the next day, they were hungry again. They encountered another beggar, this one deaf, who gave them bread.

They ate happily, but they were hungry again in the morning. But another bread-carrying beggar appeared, one who couldn't speak. And so on and so forth, seven deformed beggars in total, until the boy and girl made it out of the forest, satiated and alive.

They forgot the beggars, forgot the forest and fell in love. Life was not always under siege. They decided to be ecstatically joyous and to marry. But at their wedding, *they* appeared. The beggars. They crept out from the snow, shimmering on the precipice of the altar. The seven beggars came bearing blessings that were not like blessings at all, but instead like arrows. And they each delivered a blessing to the couple and each blessing was more frightening than the last, until the bride and groom were forced to remember those days in the forest. Forced to remember what they'd shoved down and forgotten. How their breath turned to crystal, how screams wove around the trees, how his mother, nineteen, lay motionless in the snow, how her father said "Leave her!" because they were still being hunted. How it was an unrelenting night in an unrelenting forest and the stars were like spotlights for the hunters, illuminating their every step.

How the bread, warm and magical, like hot scones, like buttered brioche, like challah French toast, was only an illusion, keeping them awake just long enough to see his mother and her brother and eventually her father turn into snow.

The bride and groom clung to each other, awash in memories and blood, and they screamed at the beggars to stop it, but the beggars wouldn't go away. They never went away again. They stayed and now they stand in shadow at their marital bedside, whispering, murmuring, as the bride and groom reach for each other in the dark, they stand by their kitchen curtains as the bride and groom eat, rustling the curtain fabric like snow. And so the bride and groom give up, give in, hunch over, knowing that their not-knowing could only ever be brief. And the beggars stand there under the altar, crystalline and malevolent, and they speak, speak, speak and they feed, feed, feed and they *bless, bless, bless.*

I.

The blind beggar's blessing: You should be old like me and have a long life like mine. I'm not blind, I'm eternal. The duration of the entire world lasts less than the blink of an eye

WHEN A WOMAN BECOMES A mistress. Slaps your face. Throws drinks in your face. Keys snatched back. Keys dug down your arm until your skin bleeds.

The mistress scenes: Japanese restaurant, long, glass bar, a single orchid, a black vase. The sashimi bright, severe. I swallow hundreds of dollars worth. I litter the table. Order more than I could ever eat. The restaurant is lined with mirrors. You eat small amounts. You keep kosher. You tell me about Tokyo. As if we'll go. You tell me about São Paulo. As if. You trace my shoulders. I rip into the fish. I watch you watch me.

Evening: a tiered hotel. Ivory. Metro Center. Washington, DC. The Capitol lit up like a cloud. I pour sake on the sheets. I dig cigarettes in your blazers. I pull you naked onto the balcony. You pay for it all silently. You pay for it with indulgence. You pay for these outbursts. You call it passion. I call it rage. You pay for it. You put your suit on in the morning. Your camel-colored coat. I stay in the room until noon. You've paid for it.

II.

The deaf beggar's blessing: You should live a good life, like mine. Be deaf to the "crying out" and "lamenting" over the world's deficiencies

THE EMAIL FROM ISAAC DOESN'T come until I get off the Metro, my phone connecting to service, the escalator pulling me to ground level. As I roll up to the crisp white buildings of Dupont Circle, I see his name in my inbox, appearing like a mirage. Our first contact in three years. A week after my trip. The message is classic Isaac; minimal, direct. The subject line: *DC next weekend.*

And then, as if it hasn't been any time at all: *I want to see you.*

My breath stops. My hand hovers over the phone. I know I should delete the email before reading another word, can hear every one of my friends and that one-time brusque, abrasive therapist screaming at me to delete, but of course I read on. *I read what Ross is publishing these days. I know it's you. I'm impressed.* A compliment. A real, honest-to-God compliment from Isaac. He never complimented. He would never offer praise, he was as harsh, as coolly indifferent with others as he was with himself. Now I can't possibly delete. But I have to. I tell myself I'll delete it once I read it on my computer, once I see it "officially," just for posterity's sake. And then I'll delete.

I get to the Aspen Institute, head to Governance Studies, my flat, gray cubicle in a flat, gray hallway. I stare at the email and don't press delete. I think about it all morning, through lunch with other research assistants, where we pretend to have friendly conversation instead of viciously sizing each other up. I've been here for too long to be much competition; research assistants are supposed to arrive, excel and immediately depart for something more spectacular. The trajectory at Aspen was two years, long enough to publish, to make connections, short enough to bear living just above the poverty line (the salaries at the think tank outrageous for Research Fellows and nonexistent for assistants). At thirty-one, I've stayed well past my expiration date, still tied to Ross, still publishing under his bylines, his grant applications, his name.

I think about my last conversation with Isaac, the drama, the eruptions, the cruelty, and try to make sense of them with his email now, with the casual, intimate *need* of the email's language (*I want to see you. I'm impressed*).

"Alexa?" one of the research assistants asks and I fumble, make efforts to jump back in. Something about Hong Kong protests, Mexico's aerospace industry. I offer feeble commentary. Ross and I research press and politics in the former Soviet Union. He tracks the calamity of journalism there, newspapers shredded by propaganda and fear. He writes about the journalists in the region who go missing, who are disappeared. They vanish across Russia and Ukraine and Belarus and Georgia. I track them, I research them. I speak the relevant languages.

I'm impressed.

I go to Ross's office in the afternoon, buzzing with electricity. If Isaac wanted to see me, did that mean that it was finally over with Tali?

Could we finally, maybe, move forward? I am thirty-one, only thirty-one (the age I'd wept over with my sister last week), but now it feels like an age with optimism, with possibility. There is time.

If Ross notices a change in my mood, he doesn't say anything. He's spinning, elated, Ukraine is collapsing and *he's* the one to talk to about it. *He's* the invite for the Sunday shows and the podcasts and the book reviews and the much-needed expertise. He tells me we need to prepare for the onslaught that's coming; to prepare for how in demand we'll be.

I try to keep up. Tension between Russia and Ukraine is worsening, relations are collapsing, a revolution in Ukraine is spreading. Protests against Russia, violent and impassioned, are heating up there again. Ross knows of two oligarchs in Dnepropetrovsk who just moved to Israel. They were threatened, the electricity in all their shopping malls cut. I ask what they'd done and Ross, impatient, says they played videos of the protesters in Kyiv in their malls. The next morning? *BOOM.* No power. The malls dark and morose. And once your electricity's cut, Russia's sending you a signal. Once the power goes out in your business, it's a threat, *you* need to go. They went to Israel, but that's a luxury not everyone has, Ross explains. To have somewhere to go.

I flash to Isaac's Pesach apartment in Jerusalem, the rose-colored tiles, the purple night sky, and then I try, desperate, (impossible), not to think about him.

Ross wants 500 words from me on the situation, a quick summation, which he can send to his queries in the evening. We'll write up and whip off to the relevant think tank blogs, to Reuters, to places highly specialized.

"Maybe an extra fifty words," Ross says. "550. Talk about the malls going out, even the rich Ukrainians fleeing, so we get the picture."

"Should I say they went to Israel?"

"They've all got houses there," Ross says. "The Jewish ones. But maybe don't say that. Sounds very 'Jews-have-all-the-money-they-all-control-the-world-y.'"

I nod and type everything up. I don't mention to Ross that I know about Jews in Ukraine, that Ross and I share this background in common. I long ago changed my name from one he would recognize (Ayala) to one that wouldn't code as Jewish (Alexa).

Ross also has an apartment in Jerusalem (driving up real estate prices for local Israelis) and he speaks Hebrew. He's Modern Orthodox, *da'ati*, went to yeshiva like I did. He knows the Jewish oligarchs in Kyiv, dines with them on work trips, even once yachted with them in Mallorca. He organizes heritage tours for American Jews (though he never knew I went on one), and he'd married early, as Orthodox Jews often do, at twenty-one, when he was living in Jerusalem. When he became a Reuters correspondent, he took his young wife to Germany and China and that's when it all fell apart, he told me. ("Fell apart?" I asked, pretending not to be elated). Traveling made her shrink inward and him burst outward. She clung to tradition while he became worldly, curious, disenchanted with religion. "It got to the point where she rented a studio in Berlin." But they were married still, four children, a suburban home in Maryland with a pool, his wife eternally pious and long-suffering, Ross eternally despising Orthodox Judaism from inside the prison.

"Why not leave?" I asked and he shrugged.

"It's such a tight community. It's how they get you."

I adored the details of Ross's ruinous marriage, hearing that he *would* leave Orthodoxy (and the woman that implicated) if he *could*. It made me a bad person, yes, maybe, (*no?*), but it filled me with righteousness. Isaac was a prisoner with Tali, he didn't want the life and the children that had sprung up between them like weeds. There must be separate bedrooms between them, there must be silent mornings, silent evenings, separate everything.

I'm impressed.

III.

The blessing from the beggar who can't speak: What I have to say is so wise, the living on Earth cannot understand it. I speak in parables, I say things you could never understand

I MET ISAAC IN TALMUD CLASS. We were fifteen, sophomores, his seat next to mine. We studied the Talmud in its original Aramaic, memorizing thousands of ancient laws for shaping a Jewish society. The day I met Isaac, we studied the tractate on killing in self-defense. The proper procedure if a thief tunnels into your house.

"If daylight is upon him," Rabbi Gamliel lectured to us, "the bloodguilt is on you if you kill him." In other words, if it was the day, he likely assumed you weren't home and wasn't intending to kill. Only to steal. "If he tunnels in at night," Rabbi Gamliel said, "you can assume he knew you were home and is prepared to kill. If you kill him then, the bloodguilt is on him."

Isaac's eyes landed on me. *If a thief tunnels into your house at night…*

A man in stealth, digging against the Babylonian earth. The one Talmudic argument I remember line-by-line, the image of the thief so sharp and strange to me. We analyzed the offshoots of the argument in class. Suppose the thief tunnels in at night, but it's a father robbing his son? Rashi, the French commentator, says a father would never kill his son, therefore his son can't kill him and claim self-defense. Suppose a son sneaks into his father's house?

"A son *would* kill his father," Isaac said. Everyone laughed. We caught eyes again. "A son would kill his father," Rabbi Gamliel said. "Correct, Isaac."

∽ ∽ ∽

ISAAC'S FATHER OWNED COAT FACTORIES all over the world and he came to high school each season in exquisite things—leather blazers, a thick camel overcoat. When we went on school ski trips, he dressed like a European, in silver and burgundy ski jackets, clothing the rest of the boys would have been embarrassed to wear, but his arrogance made it work.

Isaac invited me to his brownstone on Central Park West one Sunday afternoon after that Talmud class. The first time anyone at school had invited me to anything. My father taught math there and I attended for free, a fact everyone in my grade seemed to know. Though my parents wanted me at the yeshiva (it was prestigious, rigorous, Ivy League driven) they were also skeptical of Orthodoxy and didn't believe in God. And so while my father lectured us in geometry and advanced calculus and algebra, everyone sat there in suspicion, knowing that he was Jewish but Judas, an atheist, a fact not helped by his enthusiasm, his *reverence*, for the logic and lucidity of math.

We got to Isaac's building and stood in the doorway. Isaac said, "Can I take your coat?" and then he complimented me on it. Worn black leather to the knees, it was too thin for December but too sophisticated, too well fitted, for me to have picked anything else. It had been my mother's. Isaac slid it off my shoulders like a grown man and not a boy of fifteen.

He led me inside and introduced me to the housekeeper. She handed me, silently, a glass of lemonade.

Isaac said, "She made it herself."

He said, "My parents are in Milan."

He showed me his bedroom, with his burgundy blanket and ivory sheets. I sat down, smoothed out the blanket as I'd seen women in movies do, tracing their hands carefully down the material, until Isaac crept up and kissed me roughly. I said, pulling away, "You're a good kisser."

He laughed and made fun of my voice: "You're a good kisser."

He said, "This isn't your first time, right?" and I thought he meant kissing.

"No," I said, a lie.

"Who else?" he asked, and I didn't want to admit it, to reveal how lonely and isolated I was.

I said, "Jared and Noam Boxer and Adam." Boys we knew from other yeshivas.

"All of them?"

"All of them."

He said, "This isn't my first time either."

He said, "But I've never met a girl like you."

By the time I realized, I didn't want him to think I hadn't understood. He said, "Put your legs over my shoulders," he said, "like this." As if he was playing his father at a boardroom meeting, playing the big-deal factory owner, the overseer of coats.

When it was over, it was early evening and I had to go home for dinner.

Isaac walked me to the imposing front door, its wild oak carvings. Isaac pulled the coat out of the closet, crept up behind me and said, "Hold out your arms." He slid my arms slowly between the sleeves, draped the coat over my shoulders. He turned me around and buttoned each one to the top. As if he'd held me for an entire night.

He ran his hand over the collar of the coat, his gaze on the soft leather and then into my eyes. "I love this material."

Jared and Noam Boxer and Adam. The line haunted me for the next two years. Sex not with one boy but now four, sex when school held a seminar on the value of not touching a boy, not a handshake, until marriage. Sex when school canceled the production of *West Side Story* because parents protested over *kol isha*, the law forbidding a man to hear a woman sing, because "I Feel Pretty" was too seductive. Sex with four boys when I was asked to place four fingers under my collarbone to demonstrate how low my neckline was.

Isaac gave me flowers the following morning after *shacharit*, morning prayer, bowed as I walked by and handed them to me, and as I stared at the white roses, his group of boys, the six of them, laughed and laughed and laughed.

The boys came to me throughout the year, waited for me outside classrooms, the art studio, the parking lot where they occasionally smoked pot, wanting what Isaac had gotten so easily. My refusals were not angry, they were not flirtatious. I lowered my eyes and hurried on. They called after me like angry street vendors, "Come on, come on, come on." That was the year Isaac courted Tali, a dark, slim girl from Iran, the year he took her to a movie and she cried, elegantly, delicately, to the girls the next day because he put his arm around her shoulder, because he took her hand.

Isaac gave Tali a silver sheath for her birthday, panels of gray and sheer smoke, a charcoal satin collar. She wrapped herself in it, tiny wrists peeking out, wore it to the school trip to the Met, shone through the Greek sculptures and the Japanese Garden. Isaac added a khaki Burberry raincoat over Chanukah and then a rabbit fur stole. Her father called his father, demanding to know Isaac's intentions. *If a thief tunnels into your house in the day, you can assume he doesn't mean to kill.* Tali was forbidden to go on the winter ski trip to Ottawa until it was resolved. And all this time, whenever Isaac's parents were away, in Tokyo or Sydney or London, buying fabrics, looking at textiles, Isaac called me to come back to his white sheets and his red blanket. But on one condition: that it be a secret.

༄ ༄ ༄

HE WENT BACK AND FORTH from St. Petersburg throughout high school, to see Russian relatives and business partners. He practiced his Russian faithfully, and we studied it together, speaking in broken phrases on walks across the Hudson River and Central Park.

He told me he was determined to keep the factories in the family, determined that they would eventually be his. His father felt otherwise. Isaac was too soft, too boyish, too American. He'd collapse when it came to the hard realities of business in Russia.

"Business is the least of it," his father said. "You can't get a double espresso in Russia without bribing the woman in the café for the second shot." Isaac told me about the money his father put aside for such bribes, his father's long secret lists of men, the rapid-fire loyalties, the men who were adored by government one day and then jailed for twenty years the next. He asked me if this frightened me.

"No. I think you're perfect for it."

Isaac had cousins who owned vineyards in Georgia's ravaged, rolling hills. They had cases of Georgian wine shipped to Manhattan, thick and syrup-like. Isaac said, serving me, with the voice of his father, "Look out for the hints of oak."

He worshipped his father. He trailed after him in his meetings, wore his style of suit, his style of black-buttoned coats. He studied his father's gestures, the way he slammed down endless cups of *chai*, the way he laughed, ingratiating and then, abrupt, immediate, becoming stone-faced and serious. "Okay, now let's get to business." Nobody ever could or would cross his father.

He had sex with a distant cousin in Italy every time he went to their family factories in Milan. She had a studio with a claw-foot bathtub and they lay it in afterwards.

Isaac said, "You want to be like that girl in Italy? I see her in Milan and I never call her or anything in between."

"No," I answered.

Isaac said, running his manicured hands over my hip, his hands more well-kept than mine, "Then don't tell anyone about us."

I kept his secret. I didn't want to hate him. I wanted him to love me.

He proposed to Tali during our graduation ceremony, the ring with diamonds, jade and rubies, the lavishness a Persian custom.

I'm impressed.

IV.

The blessing of the beggar with the crooked neck: My neck isn't crooked at all. I just twist my neck to avoid inhaling and exhaling the poisonous atmospheres of the world

When I come into Aspen the next day, I don't have time to think about Isaac or if I should respond to his message (the message I told everyone I deleted). My inbox is flooded with new requests and Ross refuses to answer any of them. He's on edge. Protests in Ukraine have grown even more volatile overnight. His contacts are going silent, a sign that people and journalists are disappearing or at least being threatened with it. I ask Ross what we shouldsay—we need to have some response, we're being inundated with questions. Do we approve or disprove of the violence? Do we approve of violence in retaliation to Russia? Ross is distracted, unsure, refreshes YouTube clips on his laptop. He says it has never been this bad. He watches clips of the neighborhood he used to live in, his apartment next to the Premier Palace Hotel. The windows have been stoned, the glass littering the street.

Violence escalates and cascades out by the week's end. Crowds roam the streets in Kyiv, light up rings of fire in the Maidan. I write up 500 words for Ross and he rejects them. We're missing something, he says.

Police start shooting at the protestors. Ross says a story is emerging and we're only seeing half of it. A woman falls off her second-floor balcony, shot by a stray bullet. The Lavra, Kyiv's famous seven churches, are on fire, their gold crosses glinting in the hazy sky. Eastern Orthodox priests huddle, flee, in black robes, in purple hats. Ross insists we hold back, that we don't say a word.

Police and protestors alike throw bottles of fire, throw grenades. There's an explosion, and then a second, in the metro. Smoke floods the underground shops by the train, annihilates the seeds and the flowers and the gloves sold below the street. Protestors kiss in black ski masks, cars erupting in flames behind them. A photographer catches this moment, sells it to *The New York Times*. Everyone wants the next Kyiv photograph, the next moment of chaos captured. Everyone wants a say. Everyone but Ross.

Ross wants us to go to Kyiv and experience it for ourselves. His wife refuses (to my relief). He has his children to consider. Ross tells me we need someone on the ground, need someone with a tactile connection to the place, someone physically present we can hold on to, who can grasp some level of understanding, because he *can't* understand what we're seeing, it's just pixels and pithy TV voices, it's something real time, raw, but *flattened* by screens, by Twitter bullshit, by story *packaging*, no one actually knows what they're talking about and *Thank God, finally*, there is a contact in Kyiv who is responding. A Ukrainian journalist but he worked in Moscow for decades. Ross insists he'll be helpful, he'll provide points of much-needed clarity and no bullshit relief, the situation won't overwhelm a man like him, a man unafraid of brutality, a man seasoned by years of holding his breath, the suspension of soul and self required to report on the Kremlin. I watch Ross, open-mouthed, as he winds himself up and riles himself around, furious, frightened, until we get this God-like journalist maestro himself on the phone. Lev Antikov. We call Lev on a specific phone (he has several) and he answers after one ring, his voice calm and reserved, the tea kettle the only background noise. I don't know what I was expecting, why I imagined that he'd answer in the middle of a hail of bullets.

"Alexa, Lev, Lev, Alexa," Ross says in his curt, "serious" voice, the one he reserves for solemn occasions, the one where I imagine Ross is picturing himself on the evening news.

"Lev used to do the propaganda rounds in Russia," Ross says and Lev laughs.

"Putin is the best, his army is the best," Lev Antikov says. "Et cetera, et cetera."

"But you write it so well," Ross says. "That he's the best."

"Your boss is a flatterer," Lev Antikov says. And then, to me, to both of us, "But I do write very, very well."

We speak with Lev about the situation; Ross insists that crucial information is being held back from the West, that there are missing pieces making it impossible to click everything into place. Lev is careful, hesitant, in his responses. I envision a slight man at the other end of the phone, a faint, trimmed beard, overly intellectual, making points too fast, knocking cups over at parties, women smiling and then moving on.

Then ten minutes into our line of questions, Lev starts bargaining for his salary, and suddenly the man on the other end of the phone changes completely. His caution isn't borne of social discomfort, but of simple, savvy need. He wants more money before he'll tell us other things. He lets us know this information is expensive, and he needs to stop talking until we can agree on a price. He's shrewd. The protests are violent and he isn't afraid. He can name a high price. Ross loves this shift, sitting up straighter as Lev makes demands. Ross is happy now, happy he has a man now he can admire, a man he can trust. Lev Antikov is from another era, Ross says later, pared down, ruthless, ethical. He's not a bullshit artist, a pontificator. Ross is overwhelmed, grateful, practically in love.

We publish Lev's work quickly, in two days, under a different name. We quote him in our own work as an unnamed source. We deposit money in a specific European bank account. We move fast. Lev makes jokes. Hidden bank accounts. Secret articles. Public personas. A bad movie. He's a cliché right?

"So are we," Ross says, energized by the clichés, by the mysteries, by the secret society of information only we can access.

Then, three days later, like so many of the men I write about, Lev Antikov disappears.

༄ ༄ ༄

AFTER A WEEKEND OF FRUITLESS searching, we're told by his landlord (or a man claiming to be his landlord) that Lev met a woman and fell in love. He'd run away with a twenty-year-old oligarch's daughter and was living in her dacha by Peterhoff, wanting to be left alone.

V.

The blessing of the beggar with the hunchback: You should be like me. I have broad shoulders, which bear difficult responsibilities

THE WEDDING WAS SUPPOSED TO be at the Plaza Hotel in Midtown. I followed Tali on Instagram, shadowing every story, caption, post. She and her mother panned the Plaza in videos; three tiers of ballrooms, waiting rooms, Greek water fountains and harps. I wasn't invited, hadn't received a creamy, embossed, gold-lettered invitation, but I followed Tali voraciously, minute by minute, and I knew when a fire broke out at the Plaza Hotel one month before the wedding, and I knew that her wedding was moved to the Boathouse in Central Park.

Saturday night. Dead of December. I picked my way through Central Park in heels, stumbling through the brusque night air, the icy pathways, the naked winter trees, the Boathouse illuminated in the distance like a gingerbread house. I covered myself in a puffy pink jacket. Isaac would have hated it but there was no other choice. It was sub-zero, I was already shaking. I had nothing else, no other coat that was warmer and more elegant than this.

People arrived in chartered cars and commissioned white buses from Central Park. No one else had arrived on foot, emerging uninvited from the trees and the shrubs and the dark. My feet were bleeding in their heels. I took a welcome glass of champagne and sat down for the ceremony, the park's black lake gleaming like onyx behind the altar. There was a string quartet as the bridesmaids waltzed down the aisle in ivory and off-white. Isaac walked down with his parents, his mother and father unsmiling and austere. And then Tali emerged. Her pale blue dress enormous, heavy, engulfing her in layers of chiffon. Sapphires weighed down her neck, her ears, her wrists. Isaac never took his eyes off her. I drank more champagne. She circled him seven times, her cobalt lace veil trailing behind her. He stomped the glass, a reminder of marriage's tragic undertones, of how difficult it can be.

After the ceremony, I lingered for dinner and dancing. There was no card with my name on it, no seat for me at any table, but there were over three hundred and fifty guests, and I moved fluidly, undetected, in between them. The men gorged on steak, the women picked at salads, the children cried and the girls from my grade eyed me with confusion, with disdain. I felt hungry, lustful, the dense, corpulent catering smells seeping into my body. I wanted the steak, the meat smothered in sauce, and I waited until I saw a woman get up and leave hers unattended, and as soon as she began to dance (men and women dancing separately, a lacy fence erected in between them), I sat down in her chair and began to eat. I ate and ate and ate. I finished her steak and I began eyeing other women, other steaks, and as they got up at other tables to dance, vanishing one by one, I ate theirs as well, slicing sharply through each cut, stuffing myself with each bite, until by the end I was swallowing them by the half. I ate and ate and ate, the edible flowers, the juniper berry marinade running down my face, running down the pale pink beads of the vintage dress I wore, until I felt a furious tap on my shoulder. I looked up to see Isaac's mother, imperious, platinum blonde, a dress of charcoal gray and Swarovski crystals, staring at me with unadulterated hate.

She reached out her hand, fingernails long and silver, and motioned towards me to get up. I stood and followed her, deferential and meek. As we approached the exit, her grip tightened around my wrist and she yanked me leftwards, into a back hallway, towards the kitchen, bright, loud, and hot. She shoved me inside, the hospital-grade lighting flooding us both, and she yanked me towards the stove tops, bursting with flames. She grabbed a wok out of the young, sweaty hands of the young, sweaty chef, and despite the frozen, horrified busboys and cooks, she titled the wok towards my arm. I screamed as hot oil splashed across my skin, screamed as hot oil littered my dress. The kitchen staff stared at us, wordless, and no one moved to help. My skin burned with recognition. Only then did I notice the men that had followed us inside, two men without faces, men that stood right behind his mother and watched.

"Stay the fuck away from my son," she said. (Or did she say that? Or did his mother just look at me with satisfaction, with release? Did the men approach and usher me into the frozen park, one man on each arm, or did I limp away alone?) His mother left, the door slamming shut behind her, the crescent half-moon window vibrating (or did it shatter?).

༄ ༄ ༄

THE YEAR AFTER I STARTED at Aspen, Ross took me to Russia on our first research trip together. We arrived in St. Petersburg at ten in the morning, the winter sky still black, the sun rising, dim, uncertain, by noon.

We were invited to a party for that first night. A friend of Ross, a Jewish connection. Ross told me to dress up, and for the first time in this first year of working for him, I wondered if Ross was attracted to me, if anything would happen between us, anything in the stripped-down Russian hotel rooms we occupied side by side. I don't find Ross attractive, his anxious stature, his high-pitched voice, but I liked the way he told me how to dress—it evoked something in me, something plain, primordial. I liked the feeling that his wife would be ruined by our affair, that she would hate me, that I would be powerful enough to crush something, crush their aqua pool, their Maryland porch, their tiny golden children. I told Ross I had something to wear.

I blame that feeling of foreplay, that tiny flutter by Ross's tiny command, for what happened next. I blame it for all the years that followed from that one night.

We arrived at the party by nine and were handed flutes of champagne. A butler removed my coat, thick and lush and Chanel and blue. I couldn't afford it but I bought it anyway, pretending that I was rich. Ross told me that ten of the richest men in Russia were in that room. He whispered introductions, summaries in my ear. I smiled, calculated, took the middle-aged men in, and then Ross gestured towards a young man, sharp and slim and lean and white like a vampire. *His father "committed suicide" last year*, Ross whispered, the quotation marks implying that the death, a drowning, his father wearing a hundred coats and jumping into the Baltic Sea, was staged.

I looked across the room and made eye contact with Isaac. He gave me a half smile, tipped his flute towards mine.

"You know him?" Ross asked and I didn't want to tell Ross about the yeshiva. I never want Ross to know I'm Jewish, to know that unending part of my life. I want a clean break.

"No," I said. "We're just the only two people here under the age of fifty."

"Careful," Ross said. "He's an Orthodox Jew. We're weird. Fucked up. Believe me."

"I do."

"And his family's *very* fucked up," Ross continued. "His father was... *And* he has a wife."

I assured Ross I'd stay away. But Isaac and I made eye contact the entire night. As everyone got drunker, the circles of guests growing looser, we went off alone upstairs, to an emerald-green study. We stood by the fireplace and didn't say a word. The flames flickered and snow drifted in the wind. We kissed, Isaac tracing his hands up my arm, the scars left behind in spider webs on my skin. He told me the name of a hotel, to meet him in the lobby.

෴ ෴ ෴

"When I saw Ross was working with *you*," Isaac said at the hotel bar. "Of all people, of all places. I thought it was a sign from God."

"I never believed in God," I said.

"Didn't you?" Isaac said. "Once?"

Isaac leaned towards me, his eyes still feminine, still liquid, large, the smell of secret cigarettes still on him, the cigarettes he smoked during Shabbat, those afternoons on his balcony, the doors firmly locked so no parents could scream at the doorway, their son smoking on the holiest day of the week. That cigarette smoke still emitting from his plain white shirts, black pants, pale, skinny, cut-glass, cruel body.

"Isaac," I said.

We toasted in a hotel room with shot glasses made of ice. He poured me a vodka and I opened my mouth. The ice was immobilizing. The tables were made of mirrors. Mirror tables stacked up against each other. I ate orchids from the vase. Isaac said, "Those are expensive." The vase curled like a snake out of a basket. Petals fell out of my mouth. I'm grown up now, I told myself. I'm an adult. This affects me differently. I'm not a girl. This affects me differently.

Isaac took off his tie. Isaac took off my dress. Isaac put his hands around my throat. His violence felt like it always felt, a dreamy middle ground between right and wrong, between playacting and cruelty. Despite his status now, his fortune now, the money that made other men afraid of him, the money that buried his father in the sea, Isaac was still fourteen, clinging to his father's overcoat at meetings, calling his father at all hours, spilling hot tears at the ringing unanswered phone, and I understood now that it all came down to me; my fear, my admiration, I was the bridge between boy and tyrant, between childhood and death. He tied my hands behind my back with his tie. I remembered the choreography. He kept his suit on. Like he was pretending to be his father. It activated me, activated him, in this smoky interim we were returning to, the dream we were so familiar with, Isaac both boy and Isaac, finally, delivering on the promise of who he could be.

"Ayala," Isaac said.

I said "Alexa."

"Ayala," Isaac said, regressing, renaming me.

VI.

The blessing of the beggar with no hands: I have vast power in my hands but I do not use it in this physical world, since I need them for things far beyond this earth

Ross is angry, hysterical, pacing, after the "landlord's" call. I stay late with him after the hallway lights go dark and the night gets silent and chilly. There's nothing we can do. There's no one who will speak to us. We're shut out, in the dark, in a protected city with distorted information, like a heavily veiled bride, her face hidden under layers and layers of gauze. We sit on the thick, warm carpeting of Ross's office and drink lukewarm cups of tea, pile up plastic boxes of takeout Thai from across the street, while Ross types, dictates, rants, fumes, writes, calls, quotes, tries to fight the inevitable. We eat, drink, we don't dare imagine the places Lev could be instead.

We don't have to imagine for very long. Over the weekend, Ross uncovers a police report. There was an unnamed suicide in Lev's building. A man in his forties leapt from the window of his apartment building and was impaled on the spiky fence below. (Like Isaac's father, who drowned in the sea in a hundred layers of coats; Isaac will be here this week.)

The report says the man's daughter discovered him, had let herself in after her father missed their dinner the night before. She felt the chill the second she opened the door, smelled the milk and the meat left out, spoiling on the kitchen countertop, heard the swinging open window, the frame smashing against the wall. Ross tells me Aspen is coming down hard on him about this, that we can't touch this anymore.

VII.

The blessing of the beggar with no feet: We never know his blessing. This final section of the story remains untold until the Messiah arrives and reveals it to us, may it be speedy in our days!

I AGREE TO MEET WITH ISAAC (I was always going to agree to meet with Isaac). I respond *I'd like to see you*, trying to match his brevity, and with my eyes half shut, I click send. He responds quickly, this time over text, suggests dinner at a kosher restaurant for Sunday at eight. The plan is so established I wonder when he made the reservations, wonder if he always knew I'd say yes. I text back, *Yes*, and try to call. He doesn't answer. I want to hear his voice, hear answers, explanations. We used to call often, that wasn't a rule, like movie mistresses, the man hiding in his home office, a dinner party just out of sight, hissing *I told you to never call me first*, while his wife, chipper, oblivious, knocks outside with a glass of wine. Isaac never cared if I called, never bothered to establish boundaries around the phone, he was so frequently out of the country, so rarely with Tali to begin with, so often in touch with people she didn't know.

But there is no answer this time. It's clear we will stay with messages, staccato and brief. I try to dispel my discomfort, tell myself that a charged (important; *charged*) distance has always been our way. I try to prepare myself: Isaac hasn't changed and his clipped messages were proof of this. Nothing would change, he would stay with Tali. But I barely believe this, the counterarguments bubbling up inside of me like uncorked champagne. It has been three years. What if everything is different now?

I go with a friend to the Hirshorn Gallery on Sunday afternoon and she asks me how I am. Startled, caught off guard, I realize there's nothing I can tell her. Not about Lev or Ross or Isaac (*Yes*). I tell her everything is great. She tells me she and her husband are trying to get pregnant, and it's been over six months, and still nothing, and maybe it's time to seek treatment but maybe it isn't. We move through the circular hallways, reach an exhibit on the second floor, a video playing of a circus elephant in training. The elephant hangs his head, a rope dangling from his neck, the beast so much larger than his trainer yet so afraid of his disapproval. I saw the parallels of course, and could not tear myself away from the video, repeating itself over and over again, until my friend tells me her husband is here, they have to get dinner with his parents.

I shrug my coat on as I leave the gallery. It's new and red.

"Ayala," a voice says and I turn to face him.

A baby bursts out crying behind me, the sound all-consuming. But of course he isn't there.

ぞ ぞ ぞ

THE RESTAURANT IS EXTRAVAGANT, MORE stylish than I expected. The walls are black, the floors marble, the foyer white and stark. I'm the first to arrive, the host tells me, scanning his sheets as a waiter slides off my coat. I wonder, panicked, if Isaac will actually come. But before I can be led to our seats, he appears.

"Ayala," he says, hints of smoke on his breath.

"Isaac," I say, and he pulls me toward him. Hesitant, unsure, I lean against the knit of his sweater. He lifts my face up and he kisses me, the kiss deep, forceful, secure. The kiss is long, sensuous, almost inappropriate, a kiss like it's been three years, like it's been every day of our lives. This is so unlike Isaac, affection this public, this demonstrative, that I don't know what to say. I don't dare not have faith.

"Follow me," the waiter says, and we do.

"Any special occasion?" the waiter asks as candles are lit, as busboys fill our water glasses, as cloth napkins are draped across my lap.

"It's our anniversary," Isaac says and he takes my hand.

"Congratulations," the waiter says, while I stare at Isaac in shock.

"How many years?" the waiter asks.

"Since we were fifteen," Isaac says. "What's that American expression?"

"Childhood sweethearts."

"Sure."

The waiter disappears and brings us back two glasses of champagne. "On the house."

"Our *anniversary?*" I ask Isaac, as the waiter walks away and Isaac says, "Isn't fifteen when we met?"

I look down at my lap, and don't dare be happy. But happiness comes anyway, introduces itself in my body, starts in my heart, my chest, my breath, pulsates softly through my skin, like a hum and a kiss.

The meal is twelve tiny courses, each one a bite, a hint of something.

We discuss nothing over the meal. Isaac's business, the difficulty of maintaining his father's European contacts while making new ones of his own, the evolution of St. Petersburg, the new shipments of coats from Milan. I tell him about Ross and my new apartment, a studio. I tell him about a mutual friend's wedding back in New York. It feels thrillingly mundane, like we have years of conversation between us, like this one doesn't have to count. Neither of us mentions the last time we saw each other, my fury, my rage, the mirror I'd smashed, the fire in the bathtub; neither of us mentions the wedding, my burn scars, his Tali. I don't want to rush it, don't want to break the new glow, the spell of intimacy cast over this table. When dessert arrives, he asks where I want to go next. He's never done this before, prolonged the date after dinner, prolonged the established, worn trajectory from meal to hotel.

Without thinking, I tell him there's jazz next door. He suggests we go.

The jazz club is subterranean, the tables crammed together. It's sweaty, hot, too hot, but Isaac says he doesn't care. He takes off his sweater and now I really smell it on him, the cigarettes he's had this afternoon. He pulls me close to him, and I rub my face against the sweat and smoke of his white shirt. We sit at a table in the back, the stage partially obscured, and we kiss, a singer, a saxophone, wailing behind us. We kiss and he runs his hand up and down my leg, and he slips his hand inside me under the table. They bring us amaro, red wine, a bowl of pretzels, olives. Music plays that I can barely comprehend. I can't tell if there's a rhythm, can't understand if what I'm hearing makes sense. It's a cacophony of noise, imploding before us, like we ordered it chaotic, special delivered. The saxophone goes on and on.

The night culminates in the hotel. We had to end up back here, the hotel, the mainstay, the marker, of all our years together; there was nowhere else to go. We had to be in the hotel, even though my heart sinks when we arrive here, even though the hotel is such a reminder of who I was. The woman who comes to hotels, the scent of uncertainty, desperation on her as she rides up the elevator, the woman who rages in hotel rooms, smashing the minibar into pieces, Isaac looking in the other direction. But this time, the doorman asks Isaac if he and his wife had a nice evening, and this time Isaac says, *Yes.*

༄ ༄ ༄

WHEN WE GET TO THE hotel room, Isaac tells me he wants to smoke outside. We step out onto the balcony, twenty stories up. Isaac offers me a cigarette and though I never smoke, I say yes and I accept one from him. I want to keep us as close as possible tonight, want us to stay together inside this enchanted little bubble. We smoke, the smell settling into my hair, surrounding us like mist. We rest our hands on each other's collarbones, our throats, our chests. I feel his breath go up and down.

Isaac says, offhand, that Lev's death wasn't exactly what we thought it was.

My hand freezes, stays on his chest. Isaac moves away, puts out the cigarette.

"Lev?" I say. "What?"

"Look," Isaac says, "He was alive when he fell and he was alive when the ambulance came, even though they sent an ambulance with no oxygen. And he was alive when they got to the hospital, and he was alive when they rushed him into the elevators but the elevators got stuck in between two floors. And the lights went out and the hospital lost power, and he died in between those two floors."

"Lev?" I say again, not understanding. "But Lev is dead."

"That's true," Isaac says.

"But Lev died no matter what," I say.

"That's true," Isaac says. "Lev died regardless."

I step away and look out onto the city.

"He died between two floors?" I ask, but it still isn't clicking together. Isaac says yes, the power went out at the hospital. I ask him how that happened, and Isaac said I probably know how that happened. I can probably assume.

Isaac touches my shoulder. He says to wait here a moment. He has something for me. Isaac comes back outside with a black leather suitcase. He gives it to me and he asks me if I understand what will happen now. I'm not sure if I do. I'm still not sure if I can bring myself to.

"You understand, Ayala?"

I look out at the view below us, twenty stories up, the monuments in bright hot white stone below us, instead of giving him a response.

Isaac pushes the suitcase back in my hands. He says there's a gift for me. I ask him what's inside.

"Open it," Isaac says. "And see for yourself."

The suitcase is leather, blank and bare. I feel it between my hands, rub the materials against my palms. I'm holding on to this moment of not-knowing for as long as I can. I don't understand what I'm supposed to find when the suitcase opens. I don't want to know how much I don't know. I want to sleep in the not-knowing, I want to be blind. Whatever is in the suitcase can't be unseen, whatever is in the suitcase is bloodied and poisoned and will burn into my memory for as long as I'm alive. I don't want to know if there are gifts inside, presents for my silence, if the suitcase is stuffed, spilling over, with jewelry, with diamonds, with plane tickets, escape routes, black maps, with European currencies in brick-like stacks of hundreds.

I open the suitcase and look at Isaac and start to comprehend.

Isaac says, "Maybe it's not to your taste anymore."

Isaac says, "You're shivering."

He steps forward. "Hold out your arms."

Isaac lifts the silver coat from the suitcase, the piles of silver unfurling like a scroll, like ocean waves, like a descent. I hold out my arms with obedience. The coat falls over my shoulders, a fur collar, I remember. Isaac pulls it close around me.

"Do you remember?" Isaac asks. Tali's coat from that day at the Metropolitan Museum of Art.

"Do you?" and I understand that my acceptance is a vow of silence, that I'm supposed to smile and say, "Of course."

"Do you remember?" and I don't answer. I stand on Isaac's balcony, wrapped in the safety, and the danger, of Tali's coat.

The coat was a promise for another woman, for a girl. The coat is a ghost coat and it empties out, transparent, deflated, without secrets, against my body. I wrap my arms around Isaac. I hold him close and he relaxes, he pulls my arms closer around him and he tightens, he pulls me in. Isaac thinks that I'm afraid. But I think that I'm lucky.

I press my hands against Isaac's back and I prepare. I wonder if Tali will notice the missing coat, if she knows I'm wearing what's rightfully hers. I wonder if Tali has ever thought about me at all. I start to shudder and Isaac thinks it's fear again. I cry because I know I'm lucky. Lucky to have the luxury to choose it, to plan this final moment with him, lucky, we had this evening together, this dinner, this jazz. Lucky to be with him in a hotel, hotels are where we'd always been the most alive, where we'd been made, borne, defined. Lucky, memorials already below him, already in white, lucky, to be childhood sweethearts side by side, lucky, to have a man of my whole past, my whole present, a man a fifteen-year-old girl and a thirty-one-year-old woman would not have to renounce, would not have to face, would not have to accuse, would never have to stop loving.

NAOMI TELUSHKIN is completing a PhD in Creative Practice and Narratology at the University of New South Wales, and teaches screenwriting at the University of Canberra. She's taught creative writing at Arizona State University, the American University of Rome, and the National University of Singapore, and was a Fulbright Research-Arts Fellow for a screenwriting project in Singapore. Her short fiction has been published in Best Small Fictions, *Prairie Schooner*, and the *Mid-American Review*, among others, and her screenwriting has received grants and fellowships from Screen Australia, Screen Canberra, the Cannes Film Festival and the Sundance Film Festival.